MAGGIE SPARKS

Published by Sweet Cherry Publishing Limited
Unit 36, Vulcan House,
Vulcan Road,
Leicester, LE5 3EF
United Kingdom

First published in the UK in 2023
2023 edition

2 4 6 8 10 9 7 5 3 1

ISBN: 978-1-78226-716-4

Maggie Sparks and the School of Slime

Text by Steve Smallman
Illustrations by Esther Hernando
Designed by Brandon Mattless

www.sweetcherrypublishing.com

Printed and bound in Turkey

MAGGIE SPARKS

AND THE
SCHOOL OF
SLIME

STEVE SMALLMAN
ILLUSTRATED BY
ESTHER HERNANDO

Sweet Cherry

MAGGIE
That's me!

BAT
The coolest chameleon EVER.

MUM
Super smart. Bakes great cookies.

DAD
Writes a lot. Cannot bake cookies.

ALFIE
Stinky and
annoying.

GRANDAD
My favourite
wizard in the world!

ARTHUR
My best friend.

CHAPTER 1

Maggie Sparks was a witch. A small, curly-haired, freckle-faced witch, who was usually full of mischief and fizzing with

MAGIC!

But not today. Today she was sooooo bored!

It was Friday afternoon. Maggie was at school, in the middle of a history lesson. Mrs Staples was talking about kings or queens or the Ancient Romans or something.

Maggie was leaning back in her chair, looking up at a large greeny-brown, slimy stain on the ceiling. If she screwed her eyes up, the stain looked a bit like a lion. A lion with a fat tail and one leg missing. There were

another two stains that looked like slimy brown fried eggs. Maggie was wondering whether fat-tailed lions liked to eat slimy brown fried eggs, when Mrs Staples interrupted her.

'Maggie,' she said. 'What do you think?'

'Definitely extra-slimy brown fried eggs!' said Maggie without thinking. Everybody laughed.

'The question was "What did the Ancient Romans wear on their feet?". The answer is not "extra-slimy brown fried eggs". Pay attention, please. Stop staring at the ceiling.'

Mrs Staples looked up to where Maggie was staring. 'Oh goodness,' she said, a little too loudly. 'That stain is getting bigger by the day. The whole school is falling to bits!'

'And I keep hearing noises!' said Aadash. 'They're coming from behind the walls.'

'That is just the pipes,' said Mrs Staples, realising that she had sent the class into a panic.

'There are funny smells too,' said Alma.

'That is because we had bean casserole at lunchtime,' said Maggie.

'My grandad smokes a pipe

and makes funny smells too,' said Matthew.

Mrs Staples sighed and put her hand up – the signal for everyone to stop talking. They stopped talking straight away, but the giggling went on until home time.

Maggie walked home from school with Arthur, her best friend. Arthur always had a worried-looking face, but now he looked even more worried than usual.

'What's up, Arthur?' asked Maggie. 'You look like you've found a hedgehog in your pants!'

'Do you really think the school is falling down?' asked Arthur.

'I hope so!' said Maggie. 'Then we wouldn't have to go.'

Arthur looked very close to a panic attack. 'But Maggie!' he cried. 'School is very important. If there's no school, just think what would happen to my telescope!'

'What are you talking about, Arthur?' said Maggie.

'Well,' Arthur began, 'we have to go to school to learn how to be a grown-up. I want to be an astronaut when I grow up. If I haven't been to school, I will be a very bad astronaut. I could end up on the wrong planet by mistake. Then the aliens who live there will think I've come to invade their planet. They will start an intergalactic war. They will send spaceships with laser cannons and vaporise my bedroom. And what do I keep in my bedroom?'

'Your telescope?' said Maggie.

'YES!' cried Arthur. 'So that would get vaporised too. That's why we HAVE to go to school!'

'Don't worry, Arthur,' said Maggie. 'I'm sure our school will be fine.'

But it wasn't.

'Look!' cried Arthur's big brother, Charlie, when they got to school on Monday morning. 'The school gates are closed.'

A big crowd was gathered outside. The children were chatting excitedly. The mums, dads and carers, however, did not look excited – just confused and grumpy.

The headteacher, Mrs Sitstil, was trying to get everyone's attention. 'I'm afraid the school has been closed!' she shouted. 'A team of building experts came in this morning. They discovered ... subsidence!'

Maggie gasped. Her eyes grew wide and her mouth dropped open. Arthur looked like he might faint.

'Subsidence can be VERY dangerous,' Mrs Sitstil continued. 'The school will have to stay closed until it can be fixed. I'm sorry for the trouble, but can you please take your children back home. We'll be in touch as soon as other arrangements are made.'

Then Mrs Sitstil quickly ducked back through the gates and locked them behind her.

Maggie headed back home with Arthur and Charlie. She was

hopping up and down with excitement.

'I can't believe they found some Spy Duns!' she cried. 'I bet the Spy Duns were making those funny noises and smells, and … YUCK! Those brown stains on the ceiling were probably Spy Duns slime.'

Arthur looked at Maggie as if she had gone completely bonkers.

'Maggie, what do you think subsidence is exactly?' he asked.

'Well, I don't know *exactly* because I've never seen one. Mrs Sitstil said they are very dangerous. They make funny smells and strange noises and slimy stains on the ceiling. I expect they have big teeth. They must be quite skinny too, to be able to hide behind the walls and in the ceiling, and–'

'Maggie,' Arthur interrupted, 'it's SUBSIDENCE not "some Spy Duns"! I read about it in my *Big Book of Buildings*. Subsidence is when the ground under a building starts to sink. It can make the building fall down. That's why it's dangerous. It's not monsters living in the school!'

Maggie looked at Arthur and laughed. 'Oh, Arthur!' she said. 'You have the strangest ideas.' Then she skipped down the path, towards her front door, to tell her mum the good news.

CHAPTER 2

Maggie was at home, in her second day of online video classes, when a letter arrived from her school.

'Oh look,' said Mum. 'The school has decided to split the classes up. They are sending a few children to each of the other schools nearby, until the building is safe again.'

'But, Mum, will I still be at the same school as Arthur?' Maggie asked.

'Yes, darling, don't worry,' said Mum. 'You're both going to – oh wow! Peregrine Falconer Primary School.'

'Peregrine Falconer Primary School?!' said Maggie. 'I can't go there! The students are all posh and they have stupid school uniforms. And Alma said the teachers eat naughty children for BREAKFAST!'

'Oh, Maggie, don't be so silly,' said Mum

DING DONG

went the doorbell, before Maggie could reply.

It was Arthur.

'Have you heard the news?' said Maggie, dragging him into the house. 'We're going to Peregrine Falconer Primary School!'

'I know!' said Arthur. 'Isn't it absolutely–'

'Awful!' said Maggie.

'Brilliant!' said Arthur.

'Brilliant?' said Maggie, surprised.

'What's brilliant about it?'

'It's a brand-new school and they've got a brand-new science lab. They even have an after-school science club every Thursday. You can do experiments and everything! My big cousin Oliver goes there. He says it's great!'

Maggie had never seen Arthur look so excited.

'And do they have a magic club?' she asked sweetly. 'Or a spells club?'

'Er, no. I don't think any schools have those,' said Arthur.

'Then I'm not going,' said Maggie, 'and that's that!'

The next day, Mum bought
Maggie two Peregrine Falconer
Primary School sweatshirts. They
were a blood-red colour. The school
badge had a man on it with a serious
face and a seriously silly moustache.

'Who's that supposed to be?'
asked Maggie.

'Peregrine Falconer, I think,'
said Dad.

Maggie thought Peregrine Falconer had the same look on his face as her baby brother, Alfie, did when he was filling his nappy.

'I think the school should be called Peregrine Poo-Face Primary,' said Maggie. 'And I am definitely NOT going!'

Maggie stomped up the stairs and threw herself onto her bed. Bat, her pet chameleon, climbed onto her pillow. He gave her cheek a big, sloppy lick, to cheer her up. It didn't work.

'Oh, Bat, it's so unfair! Why do I have to go to a new school?'

Bat reached over and mopped Maggie's forehead with a tissue.

'What are you doing, Bat?' asked Maggie. 'I'm grumpy, not poorly!'

Then Maggie had a brilliant idea! 'If I were poorly, I wouldn't have to go to the new school.'

Maggie thought back to when she'd had chickenpox last year. She couldn't go to school, even though she didn't feel ill. It was brilliant! (Apart from the itching.)

'All I need is a little bit of magic!' said Maggie, leaping up and grabbing her magic wand.

Bat put his hands over his ears
and closed his eyes. Maggie gave her
wand a wiggle and chanted:

'Grotty, spotty, stinky socks.
Give me lots of chickenpox!'

POOF!

Bat opened his eyes to see a surprised-looking chicken, covered in spots, sitting on the rug.

Oh poo! thought Maggie (the spotty chicken), as Bat went to fetch Mum.

It took a while for Mum to understand what Bat was trying to tell her. But after a few minutes of arm flapping and clucking, she finally understood.

'Maggie!' cried Mum, running up the stairs. 'What have you done now?'

Mum carried Maggie downstairs and sat her on the floor. Then she took out her magic wand and said:

'Magic turn this spotty hen into Maggie Sparks again!'

POOF!

Maggie was a girl again … a spotty girl with feathers sticking out of her bottom! Alfie tried to help by pulling some of them out.

'Ouch!' cried Maggie.

'Let me have a try,' said Dad. He pulled his wand out of his sleeve and chanted:

'Vanish spots from toe to tum, and feathers leave my daughter's bum!'

POOF!

Maggie stood there, surrounded by feathers, with not a single spot in sight.

'Well done, darling!' Mum said to Dad.

Maggie trudged back up to her bedroom. Dad's spell may have worked, but hers had not. Now she would have to go to the new school in the morning.

'Bat, I'm doomed!' she cried.

CHAPTER 3

Mum woke Maggie up extra early to get ready for her first day at Peregrine "Poo-Face" Primary School.

'Are you looking forward to it?' asked Mum.

'NO!' said Maggie.

'Aren't you even a little bit excited?' asked Dad.

'NO!' said Maggie.

But it didn't matter because Arthur was excited enough for both of them. He sat in Mum's car, waving his hands and chatting non-stop, with a face like an overexcited puppy.

Maggie felt worried and grumpy and tired all at the same time. Poor Bat didn't know whether to turn Worry White or Angry Red, and ended up looking like a candy cane!

Peregrine Falconer Primary
School was a huge building. It had
long glass panels that gleamed in
the bright morning sunshine.

'It's too shiny,' grumbled Maggie.
'Our old school was much ...'

'Dirtier?' said Arthur.

'Yes,' said Maggie, 'but in a
good way!'

Mr Evans, the headteacher, came
to meet them. He was not as old
or as posh as Maggie had expected.
He actually seemed quite nice.
But Maggie was NOT falling for it!

He was clearly an evil genius, pretending to be nice.

'Good morning, Mrs Sparks,' said Mr Evans with a smile. 'And hello, Maggie and Arthur. Welcome to our school. I hope you'll be very happy here!'

I won't, thought Maggie.

'Ah!' said Mr Evans. 'Here's Miss Raven, your class teacher.'

A young woman glided towards them. She was slim and pale, with shiny black hair. Her clothes were very dark and her lipstick was very red.

'I think she's a vampire,' Maggie whispered to Arthur. 'She can't be,' Arthur whispered back. 'Vampires hate the sun and she's out in the daylight.'

'Hello, Arthur. Hello, Maggie,' said Miss Raven in a velvety voice. 'I hear that you're keen to join our science club, Arthur. Would you like to join too, Maggie?'

'That would be lovely!' said Mum before Maggie could speak.

'Excellent!' said Miss Raven. 'I run that club. We're always looking for new members.'

Maggie looked closely at Miss Raven's teeth as she talked. They looked normal, but maybe her fangs only came out at night. Arthur, meanwhile, was looking at Miss Raven with an odd little smile on his face.

Everything about Peregrine Falconer Primary was different from Maggie's old school. The classrooms were bigger. The lunch was healthier (no chips!). The playground equipment was newer. You didn't have to kick the pipes to get the hot taps to work in the toilets. There weren't even any slime patches on the ceilings!

It all felt wrong. Then it got WORSE.

At playtime, two of the girls in Maggie and Arthur's class – Eleanor and Isabella – started making nasty comments about them.

'We don't want you here,' said Isabella. 'This is *our* school!'

Then Eleanor shouted, 'Eeew! Don't go near them – they've got subsidence!'

'I heard their old school was covered in slime!' said Isabella. They screamed and ran to the other side of the playground.

Then the other children joined in. It made Maggie and Arthur feel awful.

'Don't be so silly!' Arthur shouted after them. 'It's not a disease. We haven't caught it. It's under our school.'

'That's right,' said Maggie. 'But when we do catch them, we'll send them over here to gobble you up!' She turned to Arthur. 'That told them.'

Arthur sighed and shook his head.

In the afternoon, Miss Raven asked them all to write a story about something exciting.

Arthur wrote about blasting off into space.

Maggie wrote about the Spy Duns that lived in her old school. She described how they dribbled slime onto the ceilings and gobbled up any teachers who stayed late.

In her story, the Spy Duns could breathe fire like dragons and poop fried eggs.

The afternoon went by in a blur and soon it was home time.

Mum was waiting for them in the playground. 'Hello, you two. How was your first day?'

'Different,' said Arthur.

'Sometimes "different" is good,' said Mum. 'What about you, Maggie?'

'I think our teacher is a VAMPIRE,' said Maggie.

'Oh, Maggie!' Mum laughed and bundled them into the car.

CHAPTER 4

The next day, Miss Raven had all their writing books in a big pile on her desk. 'I stayed up late last night reading all of your exciting stories!' she said.

'You see,' whispered Maggie to Arthur. 'Up late at night – definitely a vampire.'

'Arthur wrote a lovely story about being an astronaut,' said Miss Raven,

walking towards him. 'It had so
many interesting facts in it. Well
done, Arthur. You can have five
house points.' She handed Arthur
his book. Arthur smiled shyly back.

'You're blushing!'
chuckled Maggie.

'But my favourite story of all ...'
Miss Raven went on, 'was Maggie's!'

Maggie nearly fell off her chair
in shock.

'Maggie, you have such a brilliant
imagination,' said Miss Raven.
'Writing about creatures living
in your old school, it was just ...
magical! You can have ten house
points.'

Maggie was speechless.

'Now you're blushing too!' said Arthur.

Isabella and Eleanor looked on with faces like thunder.

Over the next few days, Maggie found out more things about their new school:

1. The maths lessons were hard.

2. Games were fun.

3. Miss Raven was strict! (But then, most vampires were, weren't they?)

4. The other kids were *mostly* OK.

Arthur seemed unusually happy. It was strange to see him not looking worried. It didn't take long for Maggie to realise that it was because of Miss Raven. Arthur smiled whenever he looked at her. And when she spoke to him, his face turned pink and his glasses steamed up!

The problem was, Eleanor
and Isabella had noticed too. At
playtime, they sneaked up behind
Arthur and said, 'Arthur's in lu-urve!
Arthur's in lu-urve!' Then they
marched around him singing,

'Arthur and Miss Raven, sitting in a tree, K-I-S-S-I-N-G!'

Poor Arthur went as red as a ripe strawberry! He stood there with his hands over his ears and his bottom lip trembling.

Maggie felt sorry for her best friend. But, more than that, she felt SOOOOOOO angry at Isabella and Eleanor!

Maggie could feel her magic bubbling up. Her fingers started to tingle and tiny sparks fizzed from her hair.

'BE QUIET YOU WINDBAGS!'

she shouted in a voice that echoed across the playground.

For a moment, everyone stopped talking and stood still.

Isabella and Eleanor didn't just stop talking, they couldn't talk!

They opened their mouths, but nothing came out. Then their tummies started to feel strange. They looked at each other in wide-eyed panic. The silence was broken when …

PAAAAAAAAAARP!

went Isabella.

TOOOOOOOOOOT!

went Eleanor.

Everyone started laughing.

'Told you they were windbags,' giggled Maggie.

'Thanks, Maggie,' Arthur whispered.

Miss Raven made Isabella and Eleanor sit at the back of the class, next to an open window, for the rest of the afternoon. Their voices had come back, but their bottoms were still very windy. They tried to tell everyone that it was Maggie's fault, but nobody believed them.

At the end of the day, Miss Raven said, 'I'd like everybody to bring something interesting to show-and-tell tomorrow. I can't wait to see what you all choose.'

'I don't have anything interesting to bring to show-and-tell,' said Maggie as she sat in the car on the

way home. 'I wish I had a dinosaur
bone or a robot or something.'

'I'm going to take my telescope!'
said Arthur.

'That's a good idea,' said Mum.

'Oh, I know,' said Maggie,

'I can take my magic wand!'

'That's a very bad idea, Maggie,' said Mum. 'Our magic is a secret. You'll have to think of something else.'

'That's so unfair,' grumbled Maggie.

That night, Maggie told Bat all
about her day at school, including
the bits that she hadn't told Mum
and Dad – about her very smelly
spell on Eleanor and Isabella.

'I didn't do it on purpose!' she said.
'I didn't even have my wand. I was
so cross that they were being mean
to Arthur, that the magic
burst out by itself.
But it was very funny.'
Maggie giggled.
Bat did not.

'Oh, come on, Bat. You should have seen their faces. They were tooting like trumpets all afternoon!' Bat still didn't laugh.

'OK, enough about that,'
said Maggie. 'We've got to take
something for show-and-tell
tomorrow. I don't know what to
take. Any ideas?'

Bat started rummaging around
Maggie's bedroom.

He found an
old pocket watch.
'Boring!' said
Maggie.

He found a
stripy shell.
'Boring!' she
said again.

Then he brought in a hatbox.
It was tied with a bow and had a
weird, feathery hat that Mum had
worn for a wedding in it. Mum had
called it a "fascinator" but it looked
more like a squashed pigeon.

'Better,' said Maggie, 'but still not
as interesting as my magic wand.'

Then Maggie had a brilliant idea!

'If I take the feathery hat in the hatbox, I can hide my wand underneath it. Mum will never know!' she said.

Bat crossed his arms and shook his head. This was **NOT** a good idea.

'Oh, don't be such a grump,' said Maggie. 'I'm taking my wand to school and that's that!'

That night before she got into bed, Maggie put her wand in the hatbox, covered it with the feathery hat and shut the lid.

Bat waited until he was sure
that Maggie was asleep, then he
crept over to the hatbox. He slowly
lifted up the lid and climbed
inside to look for Maggie's wand.

Bat wrestled through the puff of
feathers and grabbed the wand with
his mouth. He was just about to
climb out, when Maggie rolled over
and knocked the hatbox.

Bat fell backwards with a

BUMP!

Maggie's eyes blinked open. She saw that the hatbox lid was half off, so she sat up and pushed it firmly back down. Then she tied up the ribbon on the top.

Bat was trapped!

CHAPTER 5

The next day at school, show-and-tell went very well for Arthur.

'Oh, Arthur, what a lovely telescope,' said Miss Raven. 'I've got one at home, but it's not as nice as yours.' Arthur's smile stretched from ear to ear.

Isabella and Eleanor brought a model dinosaur that they'd made together. It was really good.

'What a wonderful dinosaur, girls!' said Miss Raven, holding it up for everyone to see.

Maggie couldn't help being impressed. She joined in as the rest of the class gave Isabella and Eleanor a big clap.

Maggie's turn was next. She untied the bow on the hatbox and lifted the lid.

'It's a dead pigeon!' someone said.

'No, it's a sort of feathery hat,' said Maggie. 'But that's not all!'

Maggie reached under the hat to pull out her magic wand. But instead of a wand, out came

… BAT! Maggie was nearly as shocked as the rest of the class to find herself holding the embarrassed-looking chameleon.

The students all thought that Bat was amazing. Bat loved being the centre of attention. Soon he was showing off, changing colours, and curling his tail up and straightening it again like a party blower.

Isabella and Eleanor's dinosaur was forgotten. Maggie couldn't help noticing how upset they looked.

'Very interesting, Maggie,' said Miss Raven. 'But you shouldn't have brought him to school. Pets are NOT allowed!'

Miss Raven asked Mrs Penpot in the office to call Maggie's dad.

Dad had to cancel a newspaper interview to come and get Bat. He was not impressed. 'What were you thinking, Maggie?' he asked. 'You know you can't take pets to school.'

'Sorry, Dad,' said Maggie, as she put Bat back into the hatbox. Then she saw her wand! She grabbed it and tucked it up her sleeve before Dad could notice.

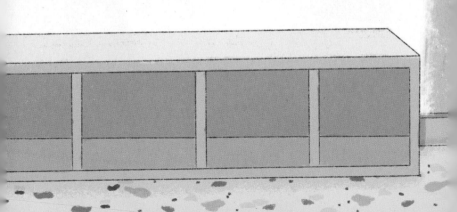

After school, it was time for science club.

Arthur was very excited, until he noticed that Isabella and Eleanor were there too.

'Don't worry, Arthur,' whispered Maggie. 'I've got my wand now. If they try anything, I'll sort them out!'

Arthur looked more worried
than happy about that.

They all put white lab coats
and goggles on.

'Today,' said Miss Raven, 'we're
going to make volcanoes!'

'OOOOOH!' went the class.

Miss Raven showed them how
to build a volcano shape around
a plastic bottle, using clay. They
worked in pairs. After a while
there were nine volcanoes sat on
metal trays, with eighteen eager
faces behind them.

'Excellent!' said Miss Raven.
'Now for the science ... First,

we add two spoonfuls of baking soda into our volcanoes. Then two drops of yellow and two drops of red food colouring. Then one spoonful of washing-up liquid. Now give it a stir.'

When everyone had finished mixing, Miss Raven clapped her hands and said, 'Time for the MAGIC ingredient.' She pulled out a bottle of clear liquid. 'Watch this!'

Miss Raven poured some of the liquid into her volcano. Orangey-pink foam started gushing out of the volcano and all down the sides, to fill the tray at the bottom.

Everyone cheered and clapped. 'It's vinegar,' said Miss Raven. 'It causes a chemical reaction when it mixes with the other ingredients.'

One by one, each pair poured vinegar into their volcano. Some fizzed more than others – some sent lava over the side of the tray.

Noah's volcano had a hole in the side, so the lava shot all over his trousers.

Soon there were just two volcanoes left to erupt: Maggie and Arthur's, and Isabella and Eleanor's.

Isabella poured the vinegar into their volcano. A tiny splodge of lava crept over the edge and dribbled down one side. It was RUBBISH! The two girls stood there almost in tears.

'What's wrong with them?' whispered Maggie.

'They're just upset,' said Arthur. 'I think they're used to being the best at everything.'

'Oh!' said Maggie. 'Well I'll show them who's the BEST at volcanoes … with just a little bit of MAGIC.'

'No!' said Arthur, but Maggie took no notice.

She took out her wand, gave it a little wiggle under the desk and whispered:

'Lava bubble, foam and fire, one stay low and one go higher!'

POOF!

Maggie poured the vinegar into their volcano, stood back and … nothing happened. Not a fizzle, not a spurt, nothing!

But then – 'What's that noise?' asked Freddy.

A low rumbling sound bounced around the classroom.

Isabella and Eleanor's volcano started to shudder. Their desk trembled. Then the whole classroom started to shake, and suddenly ...

OOOOM!

A jet of bright green slime shot up from Eleanor and Isabella's volcano. It hit the ceiling and rained over the science lab in a shower of slimy globs.

Arthur was so surprised he fell off his chair. He landed with a bump on his school bag. Maggie helped him back up.

The volcano slowly died down, and with a few last slimy burps, dribbled to a stop.

Green slime?! thought Maggie. It was supposed to be orange lava, and it was supposed to come from her volcano, NOT Isabella and Eleanor's. But even so, it was VERY funny!

Everyone was quiet for a moment. Then the whole class started clapping and laughing and cheering. Even Miss Raven was smiling, despite

being VERY confused and having
a large blob of green slime sitting
on her head. She looked like an
apple-flavoured ice cream.

But Arthur wasn't laughing.
He was holding his telescope and
looking as if his heart were broken …

It was, and so was his telescope! It had
been in his school bag when he'd fallen
on it, and was now broken in two.

Isabella and Eleanor walked over. They looked different – not mean anymore.

'Sorry about your telescope,' said Eleanor.

'Hope you can mend it,' said Isabella.

Arthur couldn't speak.

'Thanks,' Maggie said to them, sadly. Then she led Arthur outside. It was getting dark. Clouds had gathered in the sky and a light drizzle was falling.

'Hello,' said Mum, as they climbed into the car. 'Oh dear! What's wrong with you two?'

'Arthur's telescope is broken,'
said Maggie, holding back tears.
'And it's all my fault!'

'Don't worry,' said Mum.
'I know someone who can fix it!'

She phoned Arthur's mum to say that they would be late home. Then Mum drove them straight to Grandad Sparks's cottage.

Grandad Sparks invited them in and made them all hot chocolate. Then he took Arthur's broken telescope off to his workshop.

'Can he really mend telescopes?' asked Arthur.

'He can do anything!' said Maggie.

They had just finished their hot chocolates when Grandad Sparks came back into the room, holding Arthur's telescope.

'It looks as good as new!' said Arthur.

'Oh, it's better than that,' said Grandad Sparks with a wink. 'Why don't you give it a try?'

'But it's raining. I won't see anything,' said Arthur.

'Just try it,' said Grandad Sparks, opening the window.

Arthur held the telescope up to his eye and nearly fell over in surprise. He could see all the stars shining brightly, right through the clouds!

'That's ... MAGIC!' said Arthur
with a grin.

'Yes, I suppose it is!' said Grandad
Sparks. Everybody laughed.

On the way home, Mum drove past their old school. But it wasn't there anymore! There was just a smoking pile of rubble, surrounded by firemen.

'What happened to our school?' asked Arthur.

'Nobody knows,' said Mum. 'The whole building has fallen down, but at least nobody was hurt.'

'I know what happened,' said Maggie. 'That's what you get when you try to remove slimy, fire-breathing SPY DUNS from your school! It doesn't matter though. Our new school is much better.'

Continue the magic in ...

MAGGIE SPARKS

AND THE
ALIEN
INVASION